MOONBEAM
AT THE
ROCKET PORT

**SELMA AND JACK
WASSERMANN**

**ILLUSTRATIONS
GEORGE ROHRER**

BENEFIC PRESS · CHICAGO

Publishing Division of Beckley-Cardy Company

Atlanta   Dallas   Long Beach   Portland

The Moonbeam Books

Contents

"Where Are You, Moonbeam?"

This is the rocket port.

See the rockets!

One day men will go to the moon
in rockets.

This is Scott.

Scott works at the rocket port.

Scott will not go to the moon.

He will help the men to go.

"This is the day, Joe," said Scott.

"This is the day the chimp comes.

I will go to get her now."

"Can I go with you?" said Joe.

"Come on!" said Scott.

"What will you do with the chimp?"
said Joe.

"We want to find out what it is
like on the moon," said Scott.

"One day the chimp will go
to the moon," said Scott.

"We will see what it is like for the
chimp to go to the moon.

Then men can go to the moon, too."

"Here we are," said Joe.

The two men jumped down.

"Listen!" said Scott.

"The chimp will be here soon."

The two men looked up and down.
"Do you see the chimp?" said Scott.
"I can not see the chimp," said Joe.
"The chimp is not here."

"Look!" said Scott.

"Here comes Mr. Green."

"Moonbeam, the chimp, was with me,"
said Mr. Green.

"Now I can not find her."

"We will look for her," said Scott.

The men looked.

"Come here, Moonbeam," said Joe.

"Where are you, Moonbeam?"
said Scott.

The men looked up and down.
They looked and looked.
They did not find Moonbeam.
Where was Moonbeam?

Men looked out.

"What is this?" they said.

"We want to go on."

"We have to find Moonbeam,
the chimp," said Mr. Green.

"Then we can go."

Moonbeam and Scott

"Look!" said Joe.

"Moonbeam!" said Mr. Green.

"She likes to eat," said Scott.

"She eats and eats and eats!"
said Mr. Green.

Moonbeam looked at Scott.

"Hoon! Hoon!" she said.

Then she jumped on Scott.

The men laughed.

"Moonbeam likes you,"
Mr. Green said to Scott.
Mr. Green looked at Moonbeam.
"Be good, Moonbeam," he said.
Then he went away.

Moonbeam looked at Scott.

"Hoon! Hoon!" went Moonbeam.

"Good!" said Scott.

"I like you, too."

"Look, Moonbeam!" said Scott.
"This is the rocket port.
You will like it here at the port."
Moonbeam looked up and down
the rocket port.

"Here we are," said Scott.

He jumped out with Moonbeam.

Joe jumped out, too.

"See you soon, Moonbeam," he said.

Then he went away to work.

Scott and Moonbeam went in.

"Here is Dr. Jim," said Scott.

"He will look at you, Moonbeam."

Moonbeam looked at Dr. Jim.

Then she jumped away.

"Heen! Heen! Hon, hon, hon,"
she went.

Dr. Jim laughed.

"Dr. Jim likes you," said Scott.

"Here, Moonbeam,"
said Dr. Jim.

"I have something
for you."

Moonbeam looked
at it.

She came
to Dr. Jim for it.

"Good work, Jim,"
said Scott.

"Moonbeam see,
Moonbeam do!"
laughed Dr. Jim.

Dr. Moonbeam

Dr. Jim listened to Moonbeam.

Moonbeam listened to Scott.

Scott laughed and laughed.

"Look at Dr. Moonbeam, Jim," he said.

"Come on, Moonbeam," said Dr. Jim.

"Help me and then you can go."

Moonbeam did not help.

She listened to Dr. Jim.

"Come down here, Moonbeam,"
said Scott.

"You have to help Dr. Jim."

Moonbeam did not come down.

She listened and listened.

Moonbeam listened.

She did not like it!

She came down.

Scott and Dr. Jim laughed.

"Now we can go on," said Dr. Jim.

Dr. Jim looked Moonbeam
up and down.

He looked in to Moonbeam.

"Go AHHHH," he said.

"Hon, hon, hon," went Moonbeam.

"Hmmm," said Dr. Jim.

Then Dr. Jim looked at Scott.

"Moonbeam can go now," he said.

"Good!" said Scott.

"We will go to see General Winters."

"I will go with you," said Dr. Jim.

The two men went out with Moonbeam.

Moonbeam looked at something.

Then she listened to it.

"Come, Dr. Moonbeam," laughed Scott.

Men came up.

"This is Dr. Moonbeam, men,"
said Scott.

Moonbeam listened to the men.

"Good to see you, Dr. Moonbeam!"
said the men.

Then they laughed and went away.

"I see something come," said Scott.

Moonbeam and the two men looked.

"I see it, too," said Dr. Jim.

"Hoon! Hoon!" went Moonbeam.

Something did come.

It was big!

It came and came.

Moonbeam looked at it.

"Hoon! Hoon!" she went.

Then Moonbeam jumped on it.

"Come down here!" said Scott.

"You can not do this!"

"Hoon! Hoon!" went Moonbeam.

General Winters

"We will
go to see
General Winters,"
said Dr. Jim.

"You will have
to come now,"
said Scott.

Moonbeam saw
the two men go.

She jumped down
and ran.

She wanted to be
with Scott.

"This is where General Winters
works," said Scott.
"Come, Moonbeam.
We will go in."

Moonbeam and the two men went in.

"This is Moonbeam, the chimp,"
said Scott.

"Can General Winters see her now?"

Moonbeam looked.

She wanted to go in, too.

"Come back!" said Scott and Dr. Jim.

Moonbeam went in.

Moonbeam saw General Winters.

General Winters was at work.

He did not see Moonbeam.

Scott and Dr. Jim ran in.

Moonbeam looked at General Winters.

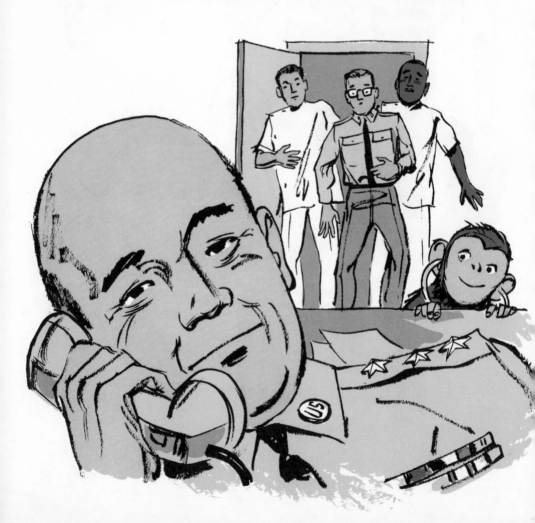

Moonbeam jumped on General Winters.

Then she listened to General Winters.

"Hoon! Hoon!" she went.

General Winters jumped.

"What is this?"
said General Winters.
Moonbeam ran away
from General Winters.
She jumped on Scott.
"This is Moonbeam," said Scott.

General Winters laughed.

"I see," he said.

"Come here, Moonbeam."

Moonbeam did not go.

"Go on, Moonbeam," said Scott.

"You have to do what General Winters wants you to do."

"Heen! Heen!" said Moonbeam.

"Come Down, Moonbeam!"

"What a chimp!" said General Winters.

"Men do what I want.

Chimps do not.

Go now, men.

I have work to do."

Moonbeam and the two men went out.

"Look!" said Scott.

"This will be something to see!

The rocket will go up soon.

We can see it go up."

"Hoon! Hoon!" went Moonbeam.

Away they went.

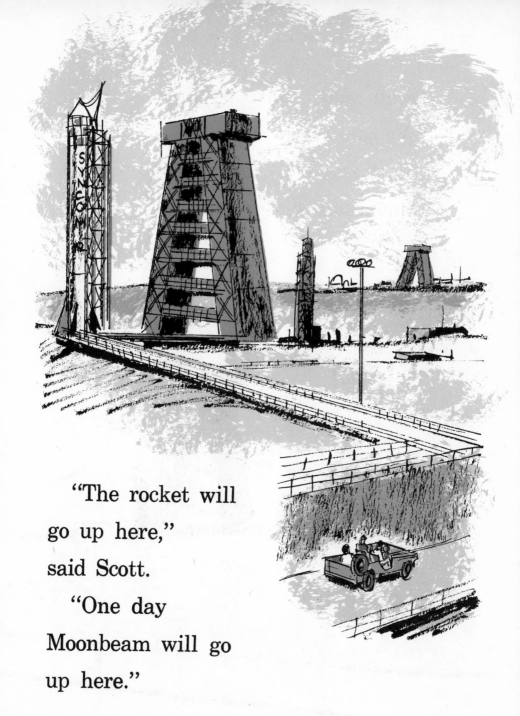

"The rocket will
go up here,"
said Scott.
"One day
Moonbeam will go
up here."

Scott said, "Here we are.
We can look now."
Scott and Dr. Jim did not go on.
Moonbeam did go on!

"Moonbeam!" said Scott.
"Come back here!"
"The rocket will go up soon!"
said Dr. Jim.

Moonbeam went on.

One man
saw Moonbeam.
"Go back!" he said.
"It is not good
for you to be here."
Moonbeam went on.
She wanted to listen.

Then Scott saw something.

"It is not good!" he said.

"Look out, Moonbeam!"

Then something came at Moonbeam.

Moonbeam did not
like it.
She jumped away.
Then she ran.
She ran up
and up and up.
"Heen! Heen!"
she went.

"Come down here,"
said one man.

Moonbeam did
not come.

"Moonbeam! Come
down!" said Dr. Jim.

Moonbeam did
not come.

"Come down now!"
said Scott.

Moonbeam did
not come.

"Heen! Heen!"
she went.

Scott Helps Moonbeam

The man said,
"I will have to go
up for her."
Up he went.

"I can not come to you, Moonbeam,"
said the man.

"You come to me."

Moonbeam did not come.

"What can we do to help?" said Dr. Jim.

Scott looked up at Moonbeam.

"I have it!" he said.

Scott ran and ran.

"Do you have something for a chimp
to eat?" he said.

He looked and looked.

Then he saw something.

"This is what she will like!"
he said.

Scott ran back with it.

He saw Dr. Jim.

"This will do it!" he said.

Then he ran to where Moonbeam was.

"I have something you like,
Moonbeam," Scott said.
"You will have to come for it!"
Moonbeam looked at Scott.
"Come on!" said Scott.
Moonbeam looked and looked.

Then she jumped for it.

She came down on Scott.

"Good chimp, Moonbeam," said Scott.

"Hoon! Hoon!" went the chimp.

Scott came down with Moonbeam.

"Good work, Scott!"
said Dr. Jim.
"We can go back
to work now," said
the men.
"Come on, Moonbeam,"
said Scott.
"We can look here."

The men worked and worked.

Moonbeam looked with Scott and Dr. Jim.

Then the men did not work.

They came away.

Then they looked back.

"Look now, Moonbeam!

Look!" said Scott.

"Three....Two...
One...NOW!"
Up, up, up,
the rocket went.
Moonbeam looked
and looked.
"Did you like
the rocket, Moonbeam?"
said Scott.
"Hoon! Hoon!"
went Moonbeam.

"One day it will be you," said Scott.
"You will go up and up, Moonbeam.
You will go away to the moon!"
"Hoon! Hoon!" went Moonbeam.

Vocabulary

The total vocabulary of this book is 71 words, excluding proper names and sound words. The 20 words in roman type should be familiar to children reading on a primer level. The 6 words above primer are shown in italic type. The number indicates the page on which the word first appears.

Are 5	help 6	*port* 5
at 6	her 7	
		rocket 5
back 39	laughed 17	
be 10	*Listen* 10	something 24
		soon 10
came 24	man 5	
chimp 7	*men* 5	Then 9
day 5	*moon* 5	two 10
do 8	now 7	
		was 12
eats 16	out 8	works 6